KU-103-698

TIMOTHÉE DE FOMBELLE

Captain Rosalie

illustrated by
ISABELLE ARSENAULT

translated by Sam Gordon

WALKER BOOKS

Captain Rosalie

014351039 5

For Jeanne
T.F.

To Molie, the biggest of little readers I know
I.A.

For Sarah, Simon and Gabriel
S.G.

This is a work of fiction. Names, characters, places and incidents are either the product of the author's imagination or, if real, used fictitiously. All statements, activities, stunts, descriptions, information and material of any other kind contained herein are included for entertainment purposes only and should not be relied on for accuracy or replicated as they may result in injury.

First published 2014 in Great Britain as a short story in *The Great War: Stories Inspired by Objects from the First World War* by Walker Books Ltd

This edition published 2019 by Walker Books Ltd 87 Vauxhall Walk, London SE11 5HJ

2 4 6 8 10 9 7 5 3 1

Text © 2014 Timothée de Fombelle

English language translation © 2014, 2018 Walker Books Ltd

Illustrations © 2018 Isabelle Arsenault

The right of Timothée de Fombelle, Sam Gordon and Isabelle Arsenault to be identified as author, translator and illustrator respectively of this work has been asserted by them in accordance with the Copyright, Designs and Patents Act 1988

This book has been typeset in New Clarendon

Printed in China

All rights reserved. No part of this book may be reproduced, transmitted or stored in an information retrieval system in any form or by any means, graphic, electronic or mechanical, including photocopying, taping and recording, without prior written permission from the publisher.

British Library Cataloguing in Publication Data: a catalogue record for this book is available from the British Library

ISBN 978-1-4063-8680-6

www.walker.co.uk

MIX
Paper from responsible sources
FSC® C144853

I have a secret.

The others think I'm drawing in my notebook when I'm sitting on the little bench underneath the coat pegs at the back of the class. They think I'm dreaming as I wait for evening to fall. And the schoolmaster passes me by as he gives dictation to the pupils.

He places his hand on my hair.

But I am a soldier on a mission. I am spying on the enemy. I am preparing my plan.

I am Captain Rosalie.

I'm disguised as a little girl, five and a half years old, with my shoes, my dress and my red hair. To go unnoticed, I don't wear a helmet or a uniform. I stay there, silent. A far as the other children are concerned, I'm the little girl who comes and sits at the back of the class and does nothing all day long.

My mother has worked at the factory since the start of the war, ever since my father went off to fight. Now I'm too old to go to the nanny's, so every morning my mother drops me beneath the sheltered part of the yard at the school for the older children, before the sun is even up.

The courtyard is deserted. I wait all by myself, eating the bread and butter that my mother has knotted into one of my father's big handkerchiefs. Dogs bark in the distance, out there by the farms. The dead leaves whistle their way across the courtyard.

The schoolmaster arrives at seven o'clock in the morning. Since coming back from the war, he's only had one arm. But he smiles as though having just the one is quite something. That and being here in the silence of the school.

"Still at your post, young lady?"

He should be calling me "Captain" and clicking his heels, but I keep quiet. Secret mission. I can't give anything away.

The master said to my mother at the start of the year that he would look after me, that he would let me sit at the back of the older children's class and do my drawing, that he would give me a notebook and some pencils.

My mother shook his hand for a very long time to show her thanks.

I hold his large bag in my lap while he opens up the school. His belongings carry the aroma of woodsmoke and coffee. This must be what it smells like in his brightly lit house just behind the school.

One of the older children, Edgar, arrives before the others, because he's always in trouble and has to light the stove in the classroom as punishment. I like Edgar a lot. I can see he doesn't listen to a thing, that he simply won't learn how to count or read, but one day I will make him a lieutenant. Edgar lets me strike the match before throwing it into the stove. The fire, when it gets going, is the same colour as my hair, like a little brother who looks like me.

When the pupils arrive, I am already sitting down at the back of the class, in my place against the wall. They are two or three years older than me. I let myself be covered by the coats as they hang them above my head without paying any attention to me. I wait a bit, and when they are all at their desks, with their backs to me, I push the coats aside as if I were bursting from the undergrowth and ambushing them from behind in a clearing.

Only Edgar notices me with my book gripped in my hand.

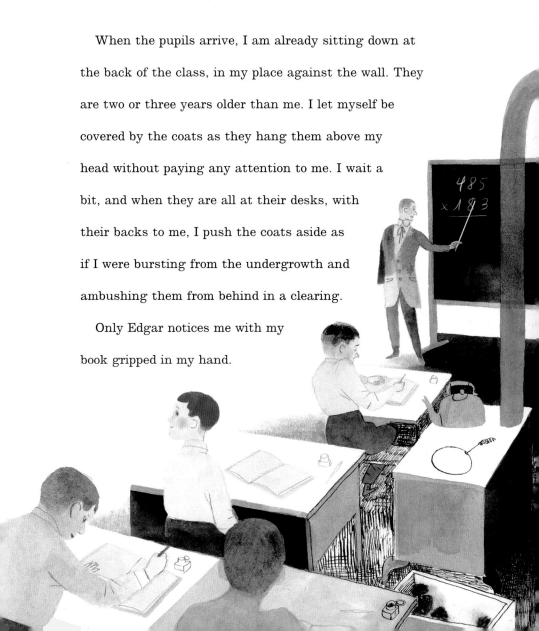

But I'm already listening to the schoolmaster, who is reading aloud from the first page of the newspaper. Every morning he tells us news of the war.

"Yesterday, Tuesday, the German troops were crushed at the Somme. Our men are fighting and reporting victories." Then he says, "We must have faith."

And then some mysterious names: Combles, Thiepval ... recaptured villages.

The master always gives us good news, never bad. He leaves the pupils standing behind their chairs a little longer, in silence. He tells them that they must think of our soldiers who are giving up their youth, their lives. Sometimes, when he speaks like that, I get the feeling that he is looking at me, and I turn away so as not to catch his eye. How could he know about my mission?

When at last the class sit down, I pretend to be elsewhere, lost in my thoughts, even though I am concentrating perfectly. I am Captain Rosalie, and I have infiltrated their squad this autumn morning in 1917. I know what I have to do. One day I'll be awarded a medal for this. It's already gleaming deep within me.

The freckles beneath my eyes, the animals I draw on the page, the long socks up to my knees ... all that is just camouflage. I have heard that soldiers hide with bracken sewn into their uniforms. My ferns are the scabs on my knees, the vacant daydreaming, the tunes I hum – a sweet little melody for a sweet little girl.

The master marks out symbols on the blackboard and the pupils recite them out loud. I watch the boy in the first row as he stands up and approaches the board.

He writes some other mystical signs. He never makes a mistake. His name is Robert, the gendarme's son. The master congratulates him and sends him back to his place. I keep a close eye on Robert. I know how important it is to spot the best soldiers and pinch their secrets.

The master whispers as he passes close by me.

"Go and get some charcoal, Rosalie. That'll keep you busy."

I stand up from my bench. The charcoal lives outside, behind the classroom, beneath the window. I cannot show that I don't want to be away.

"You can leave your book."

But I keep it in my hand. Never let the enemy seize your weapons. As soon as I reach the door,

I run through the cold towards the pile of charcoal.

I have to get back quickly. I must not abandon my post.

In the evenings, my mother comes to collect me from

the empty school. The master and the pupils have long

since left. She squeezes me in her arms and rubs her

head against mine. Lucky I'm not wearing my helmet.

I breathe in the scent of her hair. It smells good.

  "I've missed you, Rosalie."

She is very tired, and I love this tiredness. I love it when courage deserts her and her eyes are red. But very quickly she composes herself and takes my hand.

"Look!"

She brings an envelope out of her pocket. I recognize these white envelopes, covered in postmarks and black and red stamps. It's a letter from my father.

"Come, Rosalie. I'll read it to you."

As she pulls me along by my hand, no one can see anything on my face. I show nothing of my thoughts. I feel my mother's fingers clinging hard to my ink-stained hand.

"When I get home, I'm going to take Rosalie fishing."

Lying on my bed, I look at my mother side-on, the letter perched in her lap.

"I thought about the stream below the mill. I saw some

trout leaping there before the war. Rosalie will learn to

swim. Do you have that recipe for trout with walnuts?

Can you be sure that there are some walnuts left for it if

I come home in the spring?"

I close my eyes. I don't like all this stuff. My mother

keeps reading.

"My darling, I am thinking of you. I know that Rosalie is a good girl. And that the schoolmaster is happy to have her and help her. And as for you, I know your work is tiring. You'd like to spend more time with your little girl. But every time I load a shell into the cannon, I say to myself that maybe it was you who made it at the factory. It's like you are at my side in battle. Yes, the women are helping us by working so hard in the factories, and the children keep us going by lending their mothers support and being good."

I try not to listen. Anyway, I couldn't care less about being good. I don't lend my mother to anyone. I don't want to hear any talk of fish leaping in streams. I don't believe in stories of walnuts and mills.

Not one memory other than war. I was too young before it.

And I can see that my mother is still reading, for a long time, although there is just a single page of writing in the envelope. I can see that she carries on even when the candle stops flickering in the bedroom.

She shows me a drawing on the back of the sheet of paper, lines of charcoal depicting a landscape. It's the only thing that seems true. A forest in the distance and the land in the foreground all churned up, with soldiers hiding in holes. I can tell my father's way of drawing. I have seen him three times when he's been home on leave to have a rest from the war. He hardly spoke, but he held me tight in his arms and he drew horses in the mist on the window.

I fall asleep thinking of horses streaming down
the glass.

In bed, I dream of a medal being attached to my
nightdress. I dream of a general placing his hand on
my shoulder. I feel the coldness of the medal against
my skin.

Each day my mission gains ground. Each day I,
Captain Rosalie, am at my post, at the back of the class,
ready for a surprise attack beneath the coats.

I look at the inscriptions on the blackboard as if they
form a battle plan. I try to remember everything. I copy
little bits down in the back pages of my notebook. No one
pays me any attention. The older children have forgotten
about me. I have become a grey coat hooked amongst
the others. Only the schoolmaster remembers me from

time to time. And Edgar, the dunce, my lieutenant, who throws curious looks my way. I feel he is waiting for his time to come.

In the evening, my mother comes to collect me. Sometimes she has a new letter in her pocket, sometimes not. Just that beckoning to take me into her arms, those eyes that never leave mine. I prefer this to all that talk about the trout we are going to fish for, about swimming in the stream or the jams we will make one day after picking wild raspberries. The letters stay in the toffee box, on top of the shelves in the kitchen. They're better up there.

The weeks are very alike. Sometimes, at night, I open my window and lean out to listen. To listen carefully. I wonder if I might hear the noise of the war, way off in the distance, beyond the dogs at the farms.

And then one day, on my birthday, I am given snow.
Snow up to above my ankles. I can barely open the
door in the morning. I let out a cry at the flakes falling
all around.

My mother doesn't go to the factory that day because
it is snowing too heavily. I stay with her at home. This is
surely the greatest day of my life. We play hide-and-seek in
the house. She doesn't even get dressed. I find her curled up
in bed, still wearing her nightdress. She startles me. I forget
about Captain Rosalie. I almost forget about my father.

My mother rolls me up in a blanket, laughing. Since there is nothing to eat and we cannot go out, we drink milk sweetened with sugar. We cuddle together in the same armchair opposite the fireplace.

I watch the red-headed flames as they dance. Then she climbs up to fetch the big cloth on top of the wardrobe. She brings out her wedding dress. She shows me that it still suits her.

"It's just a little tight here – look."

She laughs again. Before nightfall, dressed in white, she tells me a true story with desert islands and princesses.

But later, in my sleep, I hear a knock on the windowpane.
I hear someone speaking to my mother in the next-door
room. I don't fully manage to wake up. A man has come to
tell her something. I recognize the voice of the gendarme.
My eyes stay screwed shut. And then I hear a cry. A cry
that is very long and very low, a cry that is part stifled.
But I cannot tell whether I'm dreaming or if it's real.

The following day, it's clear that nothing will ever
be like before. There's a blue envelope in the kitchen.
I cannot meet my mother's eye and she retreats when I
go near her. She talks quickly and her head is lowered.
I already have my woollen bonnet and my coat. I look at her.
She is fretting, as if she were late, yet she does nothing.
She picks up the envelope as she passes and makes it
disappear. She rolls the wedding dress into a ball and stuffs

it back on top of the wardrobe. She offers me her hand, takes me outside, her face hidden in her shawl. The snow is already melting. It will be muddy in the schoolyard.

For a month I have lived in the memory of that night after the snow. My mother still cannot bring herself to look at me. She has changed. When she drops me at school in the morning, I'm almost relieved to see her go. She walks off, shuffling, even though the ground is no longer at all slippery.

I must act quickly. *We're counting on you, Captain.* I prepare everything so I'm ready when my day comes.

And finally that day does come. It is a sunny morning in February. At the back of the class, I make every effort to follow the chalk across the blackboard. Nothing gets past me. Every movement of the master's hand. He turns round, shaking the white dust from his sleeve.

I look again at the board. For the first time, it all becomes clear. Like a fog that suddenly lifts, making everything appear. My mission is nearly complete.

I must not wait any longer. This is the moment. I am ready. I think of the medal I saw in my dream. It all becomes possible. Now I must fight out in the open.

"Young lady?"

The master is in front of me. I had not even realized
that my hand was raised. It's the first time. I've never
asked anything until now.

I explain that I left my notebook at home. I want to go
and get it. The master says that's not allowed.

I look at him seriously. I sit up very straight, my eyes
trained on him.

"It's just at the end of the road. I know the way."

"You can take a sheet of paper."

"I need my notebook."

"No. You are staying here."

His tone is abrupt.

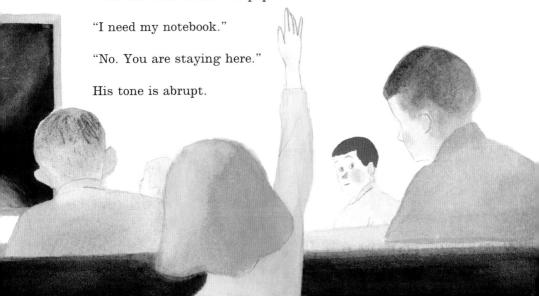

I bring out my second weapon before he has time to turn away. My gaze suddenly drops to my shoes. And there is already a tear forming between my eyelashes.

This time, the blow seems to find its target. Panic in the enemy ranks. The lines cannot hold for much longer when faced with a crying little girl. But I need reinforcements.

A voice rings out just beside me.

"I can go with her."

It's Edgar. He seems so well behaved I hardly recognize him.

The master hesitates. I wipe away my tears with my fist. He nervously rubs his hand, still covered in chalk, on the pocket of his overgarment.

"Very well."

He looks at me. Then Edgar. Then back at me.

"You have ten minutes. I don't approve of pupils
taking off like this."

I walk down the street with my lieutenant behind me.
The village is deserted. Wet rooftops shine beneath a
cold sun. Smoke drifts from the chimney of the bakery.
What is there to say a war is going on? The fighting is
so far from us. There are birds playing around the
church's bell tower. I see them skimming past the chimes.

Our patrol arrives in front of the house.

"Here we are."

"Is it open?" Edgar asks.

I take the key from its hiding place in the lizard's hole, to the left of the door. I'm not even scared of the lizard. I hand the key to Edgar.

"Open it, please."

The lock is old and usually the key does not turn. But Edgar opens the door easily. I point to the large stone for him to sit on.

"Wait for me. I won't be long."

He crouches next to the stone. He's my best soldier.

When I enter the house, I feel as though in that one instant I have grown up. I have never been in here by myself. I take a first step. There are only two rooms:

my bedroom, which used to be my parents' when I

was much younger, and the kitchen. That's

where my mother has slept since the war.

I push the kitchen door. I feel as though

all the objects are looking at me. Even the

clock is wondering what I'm doing there.

But still I pull a chair towards the

shelves. It groans against the floor to tell

me it doesn't agree. I climb up and take

hold of the metal box, right there

at the top. I look at it in my hands.

And the miracle happens. The box speaks to me.

I have seen it so often, sitting there mute on the table,

with its drawings of sheep resting beneath a tree, the

shepherd in the distance... This closed box starts talking.

The words come slowly.

Assorted ... sweets.

It's written there, on one line, in violet letters.

I have been fighting that for months. It was my mission. I can read.

I get down from my chair, place the box on the table and push open the lid. The envelopes are there.

I take the one on top. I open it. I am too breathless to follow my father's sloping handwriting, but I pick out the smallest words, those that jump up at my face as I lean over.

The word *rats*, the word *blood*, the word *fear*.

My mother never read me those words.

There's an underlined sentence which says *The rain here is made of metal and fire.*

And lower down, as if they had collapsed to the foot of

the page, the words *buried alive* and *butchery*.

I look for the letter where he had drawn the soldiers at the edge of the forest. Here it is. I unfold it. I look for the word *trout* and the word *stream* that my mother had read out. There's no sign of any stream, any trout, any mill. Nothing.

All that is written is *At night I cry in the mud* or *Oh, my darling, you will never see me again.*

At the end I see my name. He wrote it in lovely round letters, as if it were in a different language, as if I were from a different planet.

Give Rosalie a kiss.

"What are you doing?"

Edgar's voice. I don't turn around. He must not see his captain's tears.

"You can read?" he asks.

I jam the letters back into the box. My hands are shaking as I search for the blue envelope.

"Did you learn to read?" he says again.

"I want to find my notebook."

"You hid it under your shirt. You already had it in the classroom. We have to go. They'll find us."

I put the box back on the shelf and pull out the book that was tucked under my shirt.

I imagine metal falling from the sky, my father lying beneath the burning rain.

As we leave the house, I feel pain, but something has

opened inside me. I stop a second. I breathe in the pure, pungent air of truth.

"Why didn't you tell the master that I had the book beneath my shirt?" I ask Edgar on the way back.

He shrugs and carries on walking ahead of me.

"Because we're on the same side."

I'm back on my bench in the classroom thinking about the blue envelope. Where has it gone? It arrived the night after the snow. It knows the final secret.

There have been no letters since.

I've stopped listening to everything around me. It's the end of the morning. Lunchtime. Thinking back, I do not remember the hours that followed.

When the bell goes for break, everyone rushes to grab

their coats. I stay there, sitting through the storm.

"Are you coming?" I hear Edgar ask. I do not move. Some of the pupils start going out to the courtyard.

"If they come looking for me," I say to Edgar, "tell them I went to the stream, up by the mill."

He looks at me. The commotion continues around us.

"Do you need me?"

"I need you to tell them that I went to the stream, alright?"

He stands down.

I slip off the bench and curl into a ball. The master stamps his foot at the door.

"Get a move on! Outside."

He is already stuffing his pipe with tobacco.

"Edgar!" he yells. "I'm about to shut the door."

Edgar files out. I stay hidden under my bench.

The door slams. I can
hear my breathing in the
deserted room. After a few
seconds, I slide towards
the window, the one that
faces the street. I open it.

I pause for a moment. The sweet smell of the pipe is
coming to the pavement from the yard, along with the
cries of the children.

Eventually I scale the window and jump out onto
the street. I don't take the direction of the stream.
I run home.

I grab the key from the lizard's hole. For the first time,
I manage to open the door. The box. The letters spread
across the kitchen table. The blue envelope is not there.

I stand up. I look in the saucepans, the drawers, the cabinet by the entrance, the wardrobe. I search the pockets of my mother's clothes and amongst the papers in the big red file. Where's the letter? I no longer know what I'm doing. I look under the mattress, between the slats of the bed. I ruffle up my mother's bed. The sheets lie strewn around the room like ghosts.

And then, suddenly, I look up to the top of the wardrobe. The wedding dress, rolled up in a bundle. I climb onto the stove just next to it. I lift up the dusty robe. I cannot see a thing as I run my hand underneath.

It's there. Under the lace of the veil.

I take the square blue envelope.

I go and sit at the table. I open it.

Ministry of War.

These three words written at the top.

I only read the ones that come to me.

Madame, regret, pain, and then my

father's full name. And then seven

more words that feel like seven cannon

shots in the early evening.

Killed in action fighting for his country.

These words resound in me long into

the night. They kick up a cloud of dust.

Killed in action fighting for his country.

As for the rest, Edgar told me some while later.

The lesson resumes after break and it takes the master a moment to notice my absence. Not much different to the sense that a piece of furniture is missing from the room.

"And the little one?"

He inspects the coat pegs, walks between the rows of desks and makes the pupils stand up as if one of them might have sat on me or hidden me in his pocket. He looks under his desk.

"Sir, Edgar wants to say something."

And indeed Edgar is there with his hand up.

The master goes over to him.

"She told me something about the stream. She told me she wanted to go to the stream by the mill."

"The stream."

The master spins around, his face white. He seems to be searching for an escape route.

"My God, the stream. Put on your coats."

In an instant, everyone is outside. This might have been cause for excitement, but a deep silence reigns. The only sound is the hammering of soles across the schoolyard.

The master turns to Robert, the gendarme's son.

"You, go and find your father."

The pupils set off at the double towards the stream. It's the first time anyone has seen the master run. Darkness starts to fall. Edgar leads the troops.

When they get to the bank, they see that the water has risen. The stream is a torrent. The master is so pale he looks like a worm glistening in the shadow of the willows.

"My God!" he murmurs. "What drove her to this?"

Edgar organizes two parties. One to go upstream, the other down. The gendarme arrives with his son and the roadman. They go and investigate the wheel of the mill, which is striving to keep up with everything the current sends its way.

"What about her mother?" asks the schoolmaster. "What do we tell her mother?"

A sputtering of voices can be heard here and there
along the water.

"Rosalie! Rosalie!"

"Can she swim?"

"Rosalie!"

And everyone realizes they have never uttered my first name.

It is pitch-black when my mother arrives. She stops by
the school where a pupil is keeping watch. He tells her that
I have disappeared. She runs to the stream.

The master goes to meet her. He has
mud on his nose and in his hair.
His shoes are filled with water.

"Madame..."

He is unable to say
anything more.

My mother looks at the surface of the water.

The gendarme is back from the mill.

"She spoke of this place to a fellow pupil. Did your daughter sometimes come up here?"

My mother does not answer. The gendarme takes her by the arm and draws her to one side.

"Tell me ... is there any way that the news of her father—"

"No," says my mother, her voice weak.

"She seemed so strong..."

"I didn't tell her anything about her father."

"Sorry?"

"I haven't been able. I can't. Every evening, I try to talk to her, but..."

She looks away.

The gendarme falls silent.

Edgar steps out of the shadows. He has heard everything.

"I just wanted to say, I think I saw Rosalie at your house through the kitchen window. The door is locked from the inside."

Now there are fifty people outside the house, waiting in the darkness. My mother goes up to the window. She presses herself against the glass.

"Rosalie..." It's all my mother can say. She sees me asleep amidst the letters, my head on the table. The wax from the candle is melting onto the envelopes next to me.

"What's all that around her?" asks the master, whose forehead is resting on the windowpane.

"She can read," says Edgar, swelling with pride.

The master turns towards him, lost.

"What did you say?"

"She can read, Sir!"

"My God," he gasps.

A dull sound. The gendarme has just forced the door.

He does not want to be the first to go in.

He calls out to my mother.

She leaves the window, moving towards

him. The pupils form a guard of honour

to make way for her.

She goes in, alone, slowly.

I open my eyes. The flame of the

candle makes the kitchen look

like it's been painted gold.

I see my mother.

I sit up straight in my chair.

Her face is how I like it. Like it is

on the difficult days. She stays

on her feet, by the table.

"I wanted to know," I say.

"Yes, Rosalie."

"And now I do."

"Yes."

She steps forward,

takes me in her arms, and I cry with her.

The gendarme disperses the little crowd by the door.

Bright dots vanish into the night.

My mother takes a blue envelope from her pocket.

It is thicker, a parcel with the words *Ministry of War*

that she has already opened.

"This came today. It's for you."

I open the parcel. First there's a letter. I make out the words *Died for his country* that I already know. And then some words I don't know, like *posthumously* and *grateful compatriots*. But inside the parcel, underneath the letter, sits a heavy object in a small velvet bag.

I turn towards the window.

Edgar is outside, looking at me. I smile at him through my tears.

"It's for you," says my mother again.

I open the bag on the table.

It's a medal made of sparkling bronze with striped trimming.

Like a little fish alive in my hands.